REPTILES

Maria Koran

EYEDISCOVER

Go to **www.eyediscover.com** and enter this book's unique code.

BOOK CODE

AVJ46375

EYEDISCOVER brings you optic readalongs that support active learning.

Published by AV[2] by Weigl
350 5th Avenue, 59th Floor New York, NY 10118
Website: www.eyediscover.com

Library of Congress Cataloging-in-Publication Data available on request

ISBN 978-1-4896-8041-9 (hardcover)

Printed in Guangzhou, China
1 2 3 4 5 6 7 8 9 0 23 22 21 20 19

072019
121818

Project Coordinator: John Willis
Designer: Mandy Christiansen and Ana María Vidal

Weigl acknowledges Alamy, Shutterstock, iStock, Minden Pictures, and Getty Images as the primary image suppliers for this title.

EYEDISCOVER provides enriched content, optimized for tablet use, that supplements and complements this book. EYEDISCOVER books strive to create inspired learning and engage young minds in a total learning experience.

Watch
Video content brings each page to life.

Browse
Thumbnails make navigation simple.

Read
Follow along with text on the screen.

Listen
Hear each page read aloud.

Your EYEDISCOVER Optic Readalongs come alive with...

Audio
Listen to the entire book read aloud.

Video
High resolution videos turn each spread into an optic readalong.

OPTIMIZED FOR
- ✔ TABLETS
- ✔ WHITEBOARDS
- ✔ COMPUTERS
- ✔ AND MUCH MORE!

REPTILES

In this book, you will learn about

- what they are
- how they look
- what they do

and much more!

Reptiles are animals with dry, scaly skin. Turtles, lizards, snakes, and crocodiles are all reptiles.

Reptiles lie in the sunlight to warm up. They lie in the shade to cool off.

Reptiles hatch from eggs. Turtles can lay up to 200 eggs at a time.

Turtles and tortoises have hard shells. Their shells keep them safe from other animals.

There are many kinds of lizards. Chameleons use their long tongues to catch food.

Sea iguanas are the only lizards that swim under the ocean.

Some snakes can open their jaws very wide. They can eat animals twice their size.

Crocodiles and alligators are the biggest reptiles. They hide in the water to hunt for food.

Reptiles are important. Many eat pests such as insects or mice.

REPTILES BY THE NUMBERS

Reticulated pythons are the **longest** snakes. They can be more than **30 feet** long. (9 meters)

A **Galapagos tortoise** can live for **more than 100 years**.

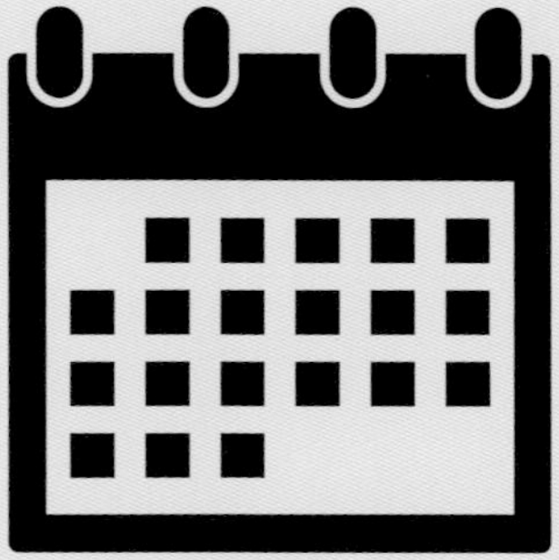

Some snakes can live for **nearly 2 years** without eating.

A dwarf gecko's body is **less** than 1 inch long. (2.5 centimeters)

A **saltwater crocodile** can weigh more than **2,200 pounds.** (1,000 kilograms)

There are more than 8,500 different kinds of reptiles.

KEY WORDS

Research has shown that as much as 65 percent of all written material published in English is made up of 300 words. These 300 words cannot be taught using pictures or learned by sounding them out. They must be recognized by sight. This book contains 43 common sight words to help young readers improve their reading fluency and comprehension. This book also teaches young readers several important content words, such as proper nouns. These words are paired with pictures to aid in learning and improve understanding.

Page	Sight Words First Appearance
4	all, and, animals, are, with
7	in, off, the, they, to, up
8	a, at, can, from, time
11	hard, have, keep, other, their, them
12	food, kinds, long, many, of, there, use
15	only, sea, that, under
17	eat, open, some, very
19	for, water
20	as, important, or, such

Page	Content Words First Appearance
4	crocodiles, lizards, reptiles, skin, snakes, turtles
7	shade, sunlight
8	eggs
11	shells, tortoises
12	chameleons, tongues
15	ocean, sea iguanas
17	jaws
19	alligators
20	insects, mice, pests

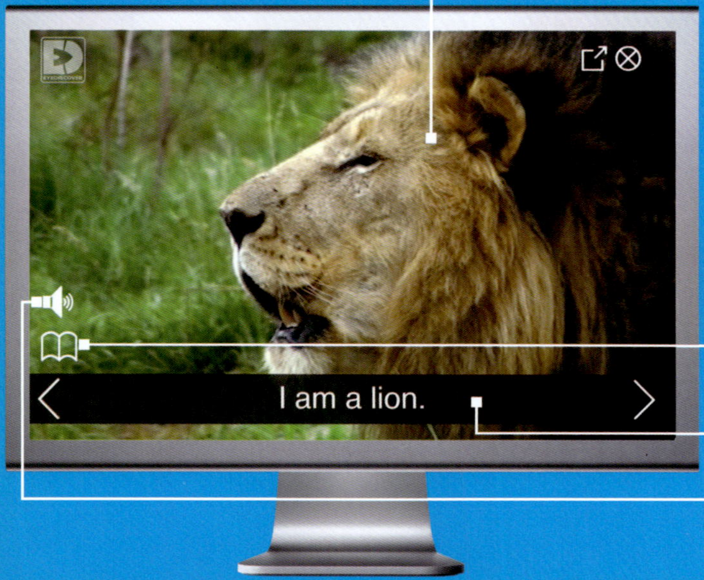

Watch
Video content brings each page to life.

Browse
Thumbnails make navigation simple.

Read
Follow along with text on the screen.

Listen
Hear each page read aloud.

EYEDISCOVER

Go to www.eyediscover.com and enter this book's unique code.

BOOK CODE

AVJ46375